Hello!

My name is Hans. Welcome to my story.

You might know me from some of your favorite stories: "The Little Mermaid," "The Princess and the Pea," or "The Ugly Duckling."

My full name is Hans Christian. But you can call me H.C. That's what my friends call me. Plus, if we shorten my name to "H.C.," we'll have more room to write our adventure.

I am a teller of stories, specifically of fairy tales. And have I got a story for you.

I was born in Odense, Denmark, on April 2, 1805. The city is southwest of Denmark's capital, Copenhagen.

When I was young, I received a magic hat. When I put my hat on my head, I am transported to marvelous places with marvelous people. Well, for the most part. There have been some not-so-marvelous people.

But every story needs a villain.

I invite you to join me on my adventures.

So grab a hat—a baseball cap, a cowboy hat, one of those hats with a tiny propeller on top! If you don't have a hat, just use your imagination. You'll be using it a lot.

P.S. If you're wondering what part of this adventure comes from my imagination and what part comes from the real world, read "The H.C. Chronicles" at the back.

GRAB YOUR
HAT
AND GET
READY FOR
AN ADVENTURE!

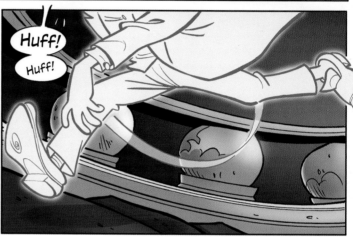

I...am very...sorry! Huff!

You can say that again, my good Andersen. We were about to offer Virginia Woolf your seat.

HA HA HAHA

?
?
?

...which makes it obvious that the man was struggling with his big nose...

HA HA HA

...as well as with his bedwetting problem which he expresses beautifully through "The Ugly Duckling."

HO HO HA HA

I think I'll be going home soon. This is just too embarrassing!

No, look, my good Andersen, there's nothing we can do. So we might as well listen to your childhood problems!

Ha, ha!

That's enough, Voltaire! I'm out of here!

5

Calm down, H.C. It's unavoidable at a lecture like this that people forget that you're only human.

But why don't you tell us about your magical childhood?

Oh yes!

Oh yes!

Please!

Very well.

You win!

It all began when I was a young boy...

I suppose I was around eight years old. Before that, I was like anyone else my age...

playful and energetic.

PLOP!

What are you doing up there, you pesky kids...?

?

Just wait 'til I get my hands on you!

I was a real rascal and never thought much about the future...

But one day something happened which changed everything...

I was visiting my grandfather...

and...

he gave me his top hat!

I couldn't wear the hat without looking like a fool, of course!

So it ended up on my drawer and stayed there...

right up until one day when I was grounded.

My mother and I had been drinking tea with my aunt. And I had accidentally smashed one of her finest teacups.

She had asked me to get the tea set from the kitchen.

There was no mistaking it. It was the set with dogs painted on it.

Auntie's eyes were as big and wide as the teacups.

My mother apologized again and again in-between Auntie's remarks that I was good for nothing.

Mother eventually promised to ground me for two weeks to make Auntie happy.

I spent the following days inside, staring out the window.

Outside,
the neighbor was hanging
the laundry.

I recall that it looked very funny,
the way she was lying there trying to
disentangle her legs from the sheet...

I decided to put on the hat.

....

Help
me!!!

H.C., help me!

How... Where did you come from... Where...?

From the bottom of the sea. H.C., you must help me.

But how can I help you? How can I even breathe?

How do I get down there?

You'll have to climb down.

I have no idea! But since you're talking, you must be doing okay.

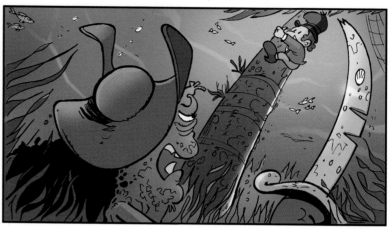

Hans Christian? Whatever are you doing?

Careful! The troll!

The troll?

He lives in a treasure box on the sunken ship, and he always gets mad when I talk to anyone else.

How dare you lay eyes on my beloved?

Hurry! Don't let him catch you!

I'll get you!

You little...

Quick, swim over here. If you can free me, I'll get us out of here.

But I'm **stuck!**

HA, HA! You'll pay for your misdeed with your blood!

I can't get loose!

Ha! Ha! **Ha!**

Hans Christian! What are **YOU** doing?

I thought you knew what being grounded meant.

But Dad?

About a week later, when I was no longer grounded, I decided to visit my grandfather. My dad had reduced my punishment...

... since I appeared to be having too much fun in my room.

Ha! Ha! Did you hear this fool? He claims he rescued a princess from a castle in his younger days.

He sounds just like your grandfather.

Hey! What's that you've got there?

My hat. My grandfather gave it to me.

Your grandfather! He's crazy! Careful, it might be contagious.

Let me try it!

Forget it! It's my hat and I happen to be in a hurry!

Where are you off to?

Grandfather's.

Your grandfather?! I told you that hat's contagious. Give it here!

And I told you to forget it! It's my hat!

Give us that hat or else...

15

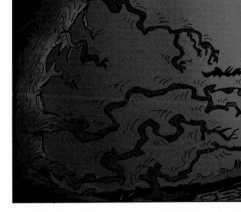

GRMMLL !

What have we here?

Who cares... as long as it tastes good.

WHAT! What is this...?

Ha, ha! We heard that children have the richest taste!

What?!?

And we're starving!

Arrg!!!

Aaahhhh!!!

Marius!

MARIUS!!!

AAAA

What
are you?

You'll understand that I was now more determined than ever to see my grandfather.

I took the hat under my arm and went on my way.

RATCHHHH !!

Hello? Anyone there?

Down here!

Hello, is that you, Hans? Come in!

He is awake, you can go on in.

Thanks, Mrs. Johansen.

3

ANDERSEN

DOK
DOK
DOK

Well, if it isn't Mr. Andersen.

It was always fun at my grandfather's. His room was full of all the strange objects he had collected.

Grandfather, what does the hat do?

You tried it on, very good. That means I'm not crazy.

What! I thought you couldn't get it to work.

Oh, yes. But I always saw the same thing. All I got from that hat was a reputation for being crazy.

Then why give it to me?

My imagination always hindered me. The hat gave me the same adventure for all the years I had it. But, Hans Christian, your imagination is special.

I don't understand...

The hat is you. It reflects your personality and imagination. When you see something that catches your fancy, the hat pulls you into your own fantasy world and your mood creates the surroundings. You have always been a kind soul. So I feel certain that you will be able to use it well.

Where did you get it?

Well... I won it in London.

I had all the winnings. I was about to leave...

when a man entered the room...

It was raining outside,
but somehow he was completely dry.

There was something familiar about him...

but I still couldn't put my
finger on it...

Good evening, gentlemen.

The others left the table in a hurry.

Without a word, we began to play.

To my surprise, I won again and again.

When he had no more money, he bet his hat.

When it landed in the middle of the table, something gripped me. I had to own it.

But after the first hand had been played, it went downhill.

I lost and lost...

... and when I finally threw my last penny on the table, he pushed the hat towards me and said:

Dear Andersen, if you want my hat, you need but ask.

Then he turned away, smiling.
He went into the cold night.

And what did I do?

I spent my very last penny.

Then I put on my top hat.

Some of my fellow sailors found me unconscious the next morning.

The ship's captain threw me in a cell. He thought I was lazy... but I wasn't!

But what should I do with the hat?

First, you must learn to use it without coming to harm.

Here, take my hand.

When you put on the hat, you must know that I am the one holding your hand.

I'm not putting that hat on again!

What nonsense is this? All that happens when you put on the hat is your imagination changes the surroundings, nothing more. If you want to learn how to use it, take my hand and put it on.

No!

Hans, instead of seeing this as a punishment...

try to see it as a gift.

Remember, I'm holding your hand.

It's just my grandfather. It's just my grandfather.

AAAAR

26

Good. Try to imagine us in a forest.

It works!

If you can control your imagination, you can experience anything. Only you set the limits.

Hee! Hee!

Ho! Ho!

But be careful. An ordinary step can seem like an abyss, and the hottest fire can seem like the coldest water.

I don't think I understand...

Here, take this piece of wood.

?

Feel it, smell it, touch the wood. Now take off your hat!

If that's not a piece of wood, I don't know what it is.

Ha! Ha! Ha!

??

But that's impossible. I could swear I felt the fresh wood, but how?

It took me a lifetime to learn the things I've showed you. I can tell you no more except to think before you use it.

That hat is not a toy!

When I went home, I tried to remember all that my grandfather had told me. I tried to remember that it was only my imagination and nothing more.

Do you want to buy some matches?

?

Who are you?

I'm no one. Are you freezing too?

Um...

That was my grandma!

Your grandma?

I lost her. She died when I was very young.

I'm sorry about your grandma.

You're the first person who has ever been nice to me.

Kiss her, you fool!

?

I bet she wasn't as beautiful as my Esméralda.

Yes, yes. Or my Juliet.

Be quiet, you two! She was the most beautiful girl I had ever seen.

As I picked up the hat, it dawned on me that I had only been talking to a small statue.

She's not real?

It was just my imagination?

You show me what I can't have and then make me fall in love with it!

I thought you were my friend? But I guess that's too much to ask for.

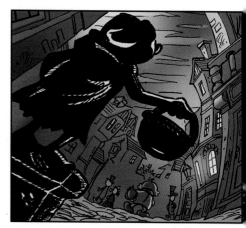

BE CAREFUL WITH THOSE, GIRL!!!

?

Look out!!!

What do you think you're doing!!! I'll make you pay for that!!!

BLUE

Mom! Look, Mom! She threw mud on my coat!

She did **what!?!**

Can you make me brave?

Help!

Now you'll pay!

SLAM

Look, Mom!

Why did you do that?

I... I can't... Are you real?

What do you mean? Of course I'm real!

I thought I'd never see you again.

I don't think I understand, but thank you for helping me.

My name is Karen.

I'm called H.C.

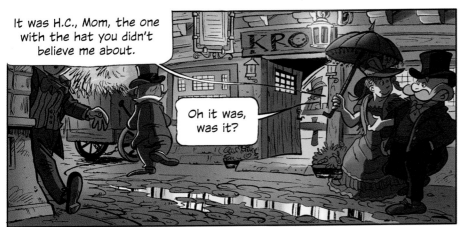

It was H.C., Mom, the one with the hat you didn't believe me about.

Oh it was, was it?

Yes, that hat is bewitched, Mom!

What is this nonsense?

It's not nonsense. I tried it on myself.

If that hat is so special, it must be worth a fortune.

Marius, you know where he lives, so you must get it for Mom!

But Mom...

No but's. I want that hat!

Meowwwwwww!

Meow!

?

Did you really think you could get away with what you did?

Let me out!

Help!!!

Ha! Ha!

Ha! Ha!

Ha! Ha! Ha!

What is this?

It's H.C. with the hat!

I only asked you to steal the hat, not H.C.!!!

But...

No but's! Put him in the basement. He can stay there until we've figured out what to do with him.

39

While I was in the basement,
the innkeeper was trying
on the hat in the kitchen.

What is this? If I don't get the gold you just
showed me, I'll turn you
into an apron!

Come and
see your
dreams,
only
10
coins.

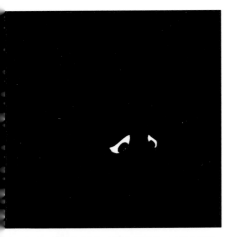

KLANK

How did you get down here?

The window.

I know this place well.

One night, I found a loose bar.

It is certainly coming in handy now!

We can't leave without my hat!

But they have it upstairs!

Then we must go upstairs!

What's so special about that old hat?

And then I explained how I had seen the mermaid, how Marius had been scared off, and how I had seen her for the first time as a little statue.

You're completely nuts.

But it's true. No matter what, I'm not leaving without it!

But it's dangerous.

Then I'll get it myself!

Fine! If that's the way it has to be, then let's get that silly old hat.

Thanks, but where could it be?

I can't imagine it would be anywhere else than in either Marius or the innkeeper's room. But there's only one way to find out.

I can see the key.

But I can't get it...

I need paper and something long, thin, and hard...

There are some old papers and a nail.

KRIK

KLINK

BLOFF

43

Yahoooo!

H.C., you're so clever!

Shhh...

Their bedrooms are upstairs.

PFF!

The lights are on.

That's Marius's room.

He's asleep!

That's right! Marius is scared of the dark. He always leaves a candle burning while he sleeps.

It's not here!

There's only one other place it could be...

RRRGRR
ZZZ

. . . . .

Shhh!

GGRRRZZ
ZZZ

47

Marius, don't let them get away.
They've got my hat!

Your hat?

Yes, **my** hat.
It'll pay for the dress
you ruined.

Follow me...

?

Not a chance!
You won't get away from
me again!

Let her go!

H.C.! Don't let go of me!

Oh no. Is that smoke?

FIRE!!!

If they're on the roof, there's nowhere else to run.

Mom! What should we do about H.C. and Karen?

Nothing, you fool!

There's no time. Put it on!

Remember, I am holding your hand.

Easy!

H.C.?

Hello there, little girl. Why so glum?

I hope it wasn't too fast?

It was great! Thanks so much.

KLING KLING

KLING

That was fantastic!

It really works. You were right!

KLING KLING

Yes! Let's get going.

KLING! KLING!

KLING KLING

N°1

53

Did the horrible innkeeper and her son escape the fire too?

Yes.

A few days after, I saw them in the street. Marius saw me...

...and told his mother.

Shut your mouth!

But what about Karen?

The last I heard, she was doing very well...

Little Match Girl LTD

That's not what I meant. What happened to you and her after all that? And between you and her?

Now that's a whole different story.

THE H.C. CHRONICLES

While my grandfather gave me a magical hat that represents my imagination, I did not imagine all of the people in this book.

You will now see the real people and places that inspired my stories.

The people and places in my stories have, in turn, inspired other stories. People have created ballets, plays, music, movies, fairy tales, and probably even some recipes.

Although my fairy tales and these other creative endeavors have been centuries and countries apart, we have all been affected by the world around us.

So be sure to open your eyes and take in everything you see. As I learned with my magical hat, even an object as bland as a piece of wood can transform into something extraordinary.

WHO'S WHO

What Shakespeare play do ghosts like best? Romeo and Ghoul-iet! Get it? Did you recognize William and any of my other ghostly companions?

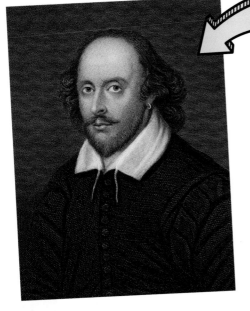

WILLIAM SHAKESPEARE

My friend William Shakespeare (1564-1616) loves talking to that skull of his. He holds it like one of his famous characters, Hamlet. William was an English playwright, poet, and actor. He wrote at least 38 plays including *King Lear, Macbeth,* and *Romeo and Juliet*. He is a *super*-old ghost. When I am with him, I feel like my young self.

VOLTAIRE

Voltaire (1694-1778) was not this man's real name. And it wasn't a case like mine of going by H.C. rather than Hans Christian. "Voltaire" was a pen name for Francois Marie Arouet. He was a French author and philosopher. Like I do in some of my fairy tales (particularly "The Snow Queen"), Voltaire's works explore the nature of good and evil.

EDGAR ALLAN POE

You might have recognized my friend Edgar Allan Poe (1809-1849) by his iconic mustache. He was an American poet, short-story writer, and literary critic. He is very famous for a poem called "The Raven."

VICTOR HUGO

Do you know the hunchback of Notre-Dame? Well, not personally. But you might know him from a movie or a book. The French writer Victor Hugo (1802-1885) created that character, along with many others. He is also famous for writing *Les Misérables.* Victor was a good friend of mine in real life, as well as in the afterlife! We even had a few adventures together!

ERNEST HEMINGWAY

Ernest Hemingway (1899-1961) was an author. He is famous for such books as *The Sun Also Rises* and *A Farewell to Arms*. He and I have a somewhat similar writing style. He had a plain, forceful style. I wrote my stories in the language of everyday life. I wanted many people to understand and enjoy them.

WHAT'S WHAT

Throughout the book, there are several references to my fairy tales. Just in case you aren't an H.C. Andersen scholar, I'll give you a lesson...

THE TINDERBOX

Remember those vicious dogs who bared their teeth? Their tongues were made of snakes? You might have tried to block that scary scene from your memory. Those dogs come from one of my tales: "The Tinderbox." A soldier comes across a witch who asks him to get, among other things, a tinderbox. He learns that when he strikes the box, good things happen to him.

THE LITTLE MERMAID

Do you remember that beautiful, blonde mermaid at the bottom of the sea? She is a character in one of my most famous fairy tales: "The Little Mermaid." You might know her from a very popular animated movie. In my story, a little mermaid gives up her beautiful voice to walk on land. This story is a favorite of many creatures—both on land and, I imagine, at sea.

One little mermaid is from my story and one is from the popular Disney movie. They both had aquatic friends.

THE LITTLE MATCH GIRL

You met Karen, the main character in my story "The Little Match Girl." My mother inspired this story. As a girl, she had to beg in the streets. I often draw on my own experiences—or the experiences of those close to me—in my work.

Here is the story: A poor, young girl walks the streets trying to sell matches. After a bit, she sits to warm herself. As she sits, she lights a match. And then another. And then another. Each time, she sees a vision, a dream. In one dream, she sees her grandmother who has died. She continues to light and light and light until she sees only her grandmother. The young girl dies. But she is happy in Heaven, reunited with her loving grandmother.

THUMBELINA

Imagine being the size of a marble or a noodle. In my story "Thumbelina"—sometimes called "Inchelina"—there is a girl so small that she sleeps in a walnut shell. One day, she meets a mean frog who wants to marry her and take her away from her shell and her mother. She runs away into the woods and, there, sees a fallen bird. She nurses the bird back to health. One day, while the friends are traveling, she finds a boy her size! They are very fond of each other and, as they often say at the end of fairy tales, they lived happily ever after.

KLING

THE SNOW QUEEN

One day, an evil troll was looking for ways to be especially evil. He created a distorted mirror, or a mirror that changed everything it reflected. Even if the kindest, most generous person in the world looked in the mirror, the mirror would reflect an image of a cruel, greedy person. In short, it projected the opposite.

All of the evil troll's friends loved this mirror. They liked to play tricks on people and see the mirror work its distortion magic. But one day, the mirror shattered. It broke into a billion pieces—both big and small—that spread across the world. Years later, one of these shards landed in the heart and eyes of a boy named Kai.

Before he was struck by these shards, Kai had a best friend. Her name was Gerda. They lived next door to each other and were as close as siblings. Kai and Gerda especially liked listening to Kai's grandmother's stories. She told of the most fantastic places filled with

the most fantastic creatures. One of these people was the Snow Queen. She ruled the snowflakes that look like bees. They were also known as "snow bees."

After the evil shards went into Kai's eyes, he changed completely. He was no longer kind and loving. Instead, he was unfriendly and wicked, particularly towards Gerda. Despite his malice, Gerda still loved him. So when he went missing, she set out in search of him.

Gerda's search for Kai lead her to a variety of characters, including a sorceress, a crow, a reindeer, and a robber. After a variety of adventures, Gerda came to the palace of the Snow Queen. After resisting the snowflakes guarding the castle, Gerda saw Kai, her Kai. Though he was not the Kai she knew. He was immobile on a frozen lake attempting to solve a puzzle. He had to use ice to form characters and words. Upon seeing him, Gerda ran to Kai and kissed him. With her kiss, he was free. He was no longer held captive by the Snow Queen. Gerda cried and her tears melted Kai's heart and burned the splinters.

From then on, Kai was kind to Gerda, for he remembered their friendship. He remembered his Gerda. The two returned home— meeting several of Gerda's helpers from the trip on the way. When Kai and Gerda returned home, it was summertime and they were grown up.

This is a story about good and evil. When the evil innkeeper was cloaked in a cape and a tiara sat atop her head, she resembled one of the characters in my fairy tale "The Snow Queen." You might know a hugely popular Disney movie called Frozen. But I bet you didn't know that the movie is based on my fairy tale.

MAGICAL MOVIE MAKEOVER

This movie was inspired by "The Snow Queen." I am so happy that my creativity inspires others. And this movie has inspired many people, especially young girls. They are as strong and empowered as the characters in the movie.

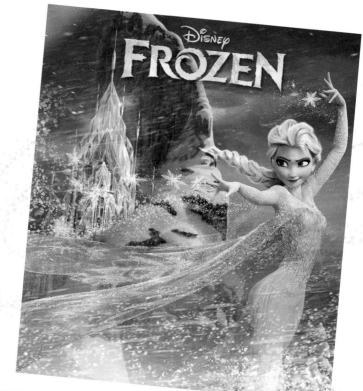

An image from the Frozen Ever After ride at Disney's Epcot theme park in Florida. That might be a good place for my next adventure!

Although *Frozen* is very different from "The Snow Queen," there are some similarities:

Animals helped both Anna and Gerda find their loved ones. In the case of "The Snow Queen," it was birds. In the case of *Frozen,* it was a snowman—a snowman who didn't know much about seasons. A reindeer aids Anna and Gerda in their quests.

In *Frozen,* Anna's heart is turned to ice. In "The Snow Queen," Kai's heart and eyes are turned to ice…in a way. He is cold towards Gerda.

KLING KLING

HANS CHRISTIAN ANDERSEN

This might be the coolest—get it, because Frozen *—fun fact yet. Some of the main characters in* Frozen *are Hans, Kristoff, Anna, and Sven. If you say those names quickly in order you get … Hans Christian Andersen. Well, not exactly. But it sounds a lot like it. If you had an idea that they would be a perfect match, let it go.*

Created and illustrated by
Thierry Capezzone

Written by
Jan Rybka

Directed by Tom Evans
Designed by Brenda Tropinski
Illustration colored by Jonas P. Sonne
Cover illustration colored by Dany
The H.C. Chronicles written by Madeline King
Photo edited by Rosalia Bledsoe
Proofread by Nathalie Strassheim
Manufacturing led by Anne Fritzinger

World Book, Inc.
180 North LaSalle Street, Suite 900
Chicago, Illinois 60601
USA

For information about other World Book print and digital publications, please go to
www.worldbook.com or call 1-800-WORLDBK (967-5325).

For information about sales to schools and libraries,
call 1-800-975-3250 (United States) or 1-800-837-5365 (Canada).

Library of Congress Cataloging-in-Publication Data for this volume has been applied for.

The Adventures of Young H.C. Andersen
ISBN: 978-0-7166-0958-2 (set, hc.)

The Adventures of Young H.C. Andersen and the Magic Hat
ISBN: 978-0-7166-0959-9 (hc.)

Also available as:
ISBN: 978-0-7166-0964-3 (e-book)

Printed in the United States of America
by CG Book Printers, North Mankato, Minnesota
1st printing March 2020

Photo credits: © Getty Images: 56 (Stock Montage), (Photo Josse/
Leemage), (Earl Theisen); Public Domain: 55, 57; © Shutterstock: 55
(Lorelyn Medina), (Aqua), 56-57 (dinvector), 60-61 (Gilda Villarreal),
62-63 (Midzumiko); © Walt Disney: 58, 62, 63.

WORLD
BOOK

www.worldbook.com